For Mum.
You might be small on the outside, but I've never known
anyone with such a BIG heart on the inside.
I don't know what I'd do without you.
Love you to the stars and beyond. xxx
—L.E.A.

Philomel Books
An imprint of Penguin Random House LLC, New York

First published in the United States of America by Philomel,
an imprint of Penguin Random House LLC, 2021.

First published in Great Britain by Bloomsbury Publishing Plc in 2021.

Copyright © 2021 by Laura Ellen Anderson.

Visit us online at penguinrandomhouse.com.

Library of Congress Cataloging-in-Publication Data is available.

Manufactured in China.

ISBN 9780593117316

1 3 5 7 9 10 8 6 4 2

Edited by Liza Kaplan. • Design by Ellice Lee.
Text set in Typography of Coop.

LAURA ELLEN ANDERSON

I DON'T WANT TO BE SMALL

PHILOMEL BOOKS

NO!

It's NOT FAIR.
I don't want to be

small.

I want to grow FASTER
so I can be tall!

I'm always on tiptoes. In crowds, I can't see!
And ALL of my friends are MUCH taller than me.

Sometimes I'm SO small they forget that I'm there . . .

THE **BEST-MOST-MEGA** ROLLER COASTER

YOU MUST BE THIS **BIG** TO RIDE

and I can't even go on
BIG rides at the fair.

My brother is lucky
for being so TALL.
He gives me his clothes
when he finds them too small.

But his clothes
are too BIG—
it's just SO unfair!

I'm so MAD, I throw Teddy Bear up in the air.

OOPS!

Now he's stuck!
Oh, what have I done?
Being this small ruins
all of my fun!

I try jumping
to reach him.

I stand on
a box.

I try stilts

and a long stick—

a rope made
of socks.

Perhaps if I eat all my greens REALLY FAST,
I'll grow **super quick** and save Teddy at last!

BURP

But NO, I'm just full, with strange sounds in my belly . . .
I'm STILL the same height, but . . . NOW SO MUCH MORE SMELLY!

Maybe I'll grow if
I'm more like a flower,

so I sit in the sunshine

and take a cold shower.

But now I'm just **wet**,
and there's **mud**
in my hair.

I will **never** be tall, and . . .

I JUST WANT

"Nice bear!" says a girl
who's much taller than me.
"Would you like me to help
get it down from that tree?"

The girl reaches up . . .
but it's still far too **high**.
"Oh dear, what a pickle."
I slump down and sigh.

But just when I think that my bear's **stuck** forever,

I gasp and say, "We could reach Teddy **together!**"

The next thing I know
I'm the **tallest** around!
I've never been SO far
away from the ground!

We laugh and
we wobble,
and then

one,

two,

three . . .

Together we finally
set my bear free!

"Thank you!" I say,
and I hold out my bear.
"Here, this is Teddy.
Perhaps we can share?"

So, yes, I am small,
but now I don't mind.

I've made a new friend,
and she's mightily kind!

We play games and laugh
for the rest of the day—

I'm small and

she's tall and . . .

we're
PERFECT
that way!